Silent Screams

The Untold Stories of Alaska's Coldest Killers and the Victims They Silenced

By D. Boone Wilder

Introduction

By *D. Boone Wilder*

Alaska is a land of astonishing beauty — a vast wilderness shaped by ancient glaciers, unforgiving storms, and silence so profound it can feel alive. But within that silence lies something else: secrets. Some are natural, hidden in the folds of snow-covered peaks or the black water of glacial rivers. Others are man-made, carved not by erosion but by violence. *This book is about the latter.*

As a former law enforcement officer who spent decades serving across the Last Frontier, I've seen both the magnificence and the menace that Alaska can harbor. I've shaken hands with heroes, walked in the footsteps of monsters, and stood at the edges of scenes that defy explanation. *Silent Screams* is a collection of true crime stories that expose the coldest killers to ever stalk this land — and the forgotten victims they silenced.

From the haunting discovery of *Eklutna Annie,* whose red boots were the only voice she had left, to the terrifying reach of Israel Keyes, whose sadistic precision stunned even seasoned investigators — these cases represent some of the darkest chapters in Alaska's history. These are not just murder stories. These are stories of girls who vanished, families who never stopped searching, communities rattled by fear, and the hard-won pursuit of justice in places where roads don't always reach.

I wrote this book not only to preserve the memory of those who were lost, but to shine a light into the dark corners of Alaska where evil tried to hide. Some of these names you may recognize. Others have faded from headlines, if they ever made them at all. But they all deserve to be remembered.

This is not a comfortable read — nor should it be. These are the stories that linger, echoing through the trees, over frozen lakes, and down lonely trails. Because in Alaska, silence is never just silence. Sometimes it screams.

D.Boone Wilder Author & Retired Law Enforcement Jamestown, Tennessee May 2025

Dedication

This book is dedicated to **Alaska State Troopers Gabriel "Gabe" Rich and Sergeant Patrick "Scott" Johnson**, who gave their lives in the line of duty on May 1, 2014, serving with honor in the remote village of Tanana, Alaska.

Their courage, commitment, and sacrifice will never be forgotten.

To those who wear the badge—past, present, and future— may this book serve as a reminder that justice is not just about catching the guilty, but remembering the innocent, honoring the fallen, and giving voice to the silenced.

Rest easy, Troopers. We've got the watch from here.

—D Boone Wilder

Table of Contents

Chapter 1: The Girl in the Red Boots

Eklutna Annie's Story

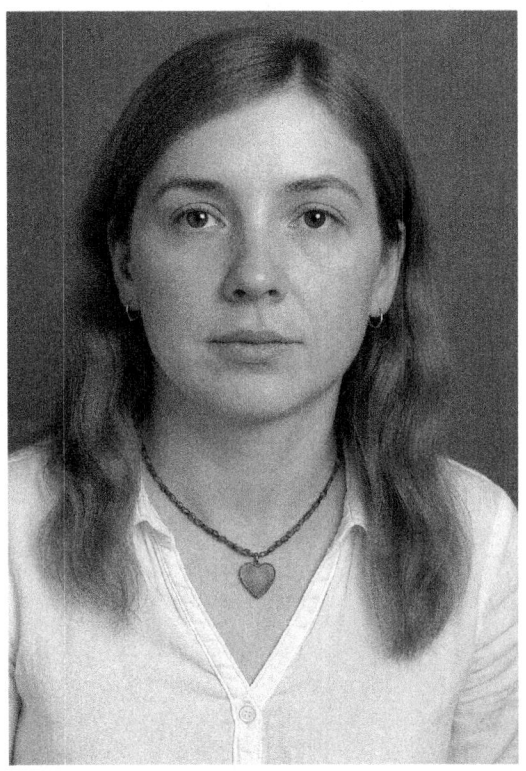

AI Generated Image of Forensic Facial Reconstruction of
'Eklutna Annie,'
an unidentified victim of
serial killer Robert Hansen

The summer of 1980 draped the Alaskan wilderness surrounding Eklutna Lake in a deceptive warmth, a fragile illusion that veiled secrets buried just beneath the thawing earth. Sunlight, a precious commodity in this northern realm, filtered through the dense canopy of spruce and birch, casting long, dancing shadows that intertwined with the persistent, high-pitched whine of mosquitoes. For the linemen of the Chugach Electric Association, the 17th of July was another day etched into the relentless rhythm of the Alaskan summer – the essential, yet monotonous, task of maintaining the skeletal network of power lines snaking through the rugged terrain. Their routine was a blend of physical exertion and wary vigilance, climbing poles, checking connections, and constantly scanning the tree line for the hulking, unpredictable presence of a grizzly bear. Here, where crude tracks laughingly called roads dissolved into muddy ruts and the dense forest pressed in like an ancient, watchful entity, nature's dominion remained absolute.

And then, amidst the familiar hum of their workday, they stumbled upon something that shattered the mundane, something profoundly and irrevocably out of place.

It wasn't the expected encounter with wildlife, though the primal fear of a bear might have been a less disturbing intrusion. It was something smaller, more fragile in its stillness, yet imbued with a chilling and absolute finality. Concealed within a shallow depression, a mere scraping of earth and tangled underbrush alongside the power line easement just off South Eklutna Lake Road, lay the skeletal remains of a young woman.

Her bones, bleached by the relentless sun and scarred by the gnawing frost of at least one unforgiving Alaskan winter, lay stark against the dark, damp earth. The skeletal structure, fragile yet stubbornly intact, whispered a silent testament to a life violently and prematurely extinguished. A faint, earthy odor, tinged with the subtle sweetness of decay, still clung to the soil around the shallow grave, a visceral reminder of the organic matter that had once been a vibrant young woman.

Her identity was a stark void, a blank space in the intricate ledger of human existence. Her story, a narrative brutally severed mid-sentence. Yet, the fragmented remnants of what she wore offered a series of stark, unsettling clues – tangible echoes of a life abruptly terminated.

A brown leather jacket, hip-length, its once supple surface now stiff and cracked from exposure, suggested a touch of practicality, perhaps even a fleeting nod to urban style jarringly out of place in this remote, untamed landscape. Beneath it, a light, knitted sleeveless shirt – its original color leached away by time and the elements, a ghostly suggestion of white, beige, or a pale, indeterminate gray, the remaining fibers brittle to the touch. Blue jeans, a ubiquitous garment offering little in the way of individual identification, clung to the skeletal frame. But then there were the boots.

Red. Knee-high. High-heeled. With zippers, like tarnished silver threads, tracing their length. Flashy. Unmistakable. The kind of footwear that would have turned heads amidst the neon-drenched sidewalks of Fourth Avenue in downtown Anchorage, a bold, defiant statement in a world of practical parkas and sturdy, earth-toned work boots. Out here, in the raw, untamed wilderness, they were a jarring anomaly, a vibrant, desperate scream swallowed by the silent, watchful trees. And she was no longer wearing them to be seen. They lay discarded a short distance away, two stark, crimson exclamation points at the abrupt and brutal end of a young life. The leather was scuffed and faded, yet the vibrant hue stubbornly persisted, a final, defiant spark of the person she once was.

Within the pocket of her brown leather jacket, investigators would later discover a small, telltale box of Salem matches, the cardboard softened and warped by moisture. A personal habit? A borrowed item? A fleeting connection to a world beyond the silent, encroaching woods? Around her delicate wrists and neck, fragments of handmade jewelry – a copper necklace strung with shell beads, their surfaces dull and pitted; a bracelet adorned with small, turquoise stones, their color muted by time; a Timex watch with a faded brown face, its hands frozen at an unknown hour, the gold plating on the hoop earrings tarnished and thin. Even a ring, crudely yet lovingly carved from shell, still clung to a skeletal finger, its delicate craftsmanship a poignant reminder of a life that valued beauty.

Now, all she possessed was a name bestowed upon her by circumstance, a stark geographical marker at the site of her tragic end: Eklutna Annie.

It wasn't her real name, a cruel irony that underscored the profound loss of identity. It was a label born of necessity, a signpost at a dead end, pointing only to the place where her journey had so violently concluded. Estimated to be between sixteen and twenty-five years old, petite in stature, standing somewhere between four-foot-eleven and five-foot-three, with light brown or perhaps a strawberry-blonde cascade of hair. The initial assessment suggested she was likely white, though the possibility of Native heritage lingered, an unanswered question in the complex tapestry of Alaska's diverse population. The stark pronouncement from the medical examiner echoed the brutal simplicity of her demise: a single, fatal stab wound to the back.

There was no identification, no purse containing the mundane yet vital details of a life – a driver's license, a crumpled photograph, a grocery list. No missing person report in the

Anchorage area, or indeed anywhere in Alaska, seemed to align with her description. Nothing. A chilling void where a life should have been documented, a deafening silence where her story should have resonated. Nothing that offered a concrete clue to who she was, why she met such a violent end in this remote location, or who had so callously left her to decompose in the cold embrace of the Alaskan wilderness.

In the vast, often unforgiving landscape of Alaska, where secrets can be swallowed whole by the sheer scale of the land, the discovery of Eklutna Annie sent ripples of unease through the community. The lack of an immediate identity amplified the tragedy, turning her into a symbol of the vulnerable lost in the immensity of the Last Frontier. As investigators began the arduous task of piecing together the fragments of her existence, a darker undercurrent began to stir, a whisper of a predator lurking in the shadows of Anchorage, a man whose name would eventually become synonymous with unimaginable horror.

Robert Hansen was a seemingly unremarkable figure in those early days, a quiet baker living a seemingly normal life. Yet, unbeknownst to the authorities grappling with the mystery of the girl in the red boots, his dark impulses had already claimed at least one life in the Alaskan wilderness. The discovery near Eklutna Lake was the first chilling note in a symphony of terror that would soon grip the state.

AI Generated Image of Robert Hansen,
aka The Butcher Baker

The connection between Eklutna Annie and Robert Hansen would not be fully realized for several years. But even in those initial days, the brutal nature of her death and the remote location hinted at a sinister motive, a darkness that transcended a simple accident or random act of violence. The red boots, so out of place in the wilderness, seemed to scream of a life that belonged somewhere else, a life tragically intercepted.

The years that followed the discovery were marked by frustration and the gnawing sense of an unsolved tragedy. Forensic teams worked tirelessly, attempting to reconstruct her face, hoping to jog a memory, to spark a recognition. Yet, Eklutna Annie remained an enigma, a ghost in the Alaskan woods.

She lies buried beneath a simple, stark marker in Anchorage Memorial Park Cemetery.

Jane Doe / Died 1980

No birthday. No hometown. No name.

Just those red boots, a poignant and enduring symbol of a vibrant life extinguished too soon, and the terrible, echoing truth of how she died, a truth that would eventually be revealed, casting a long shadow over the wilderness that became her unmarked grave.

There are cold places on this earth, vast and unforgiving in their natural indifference. But none, perhaps, are as profoundly cold as the empty space where a young girl's name is forgotten, her story silenced by the brutal echoes of the wilderness.

—*D. Boone Wilder*

Chapter 2: The Butcher Baker Story

The Robert Hansen Murders

AI Generated Image of Robert Hansen

He could have been the genial man behind the bakery counter, the one who slid a warm, glazed donut into your bag with a friendly smile and a genuine inquiry about your weekend. Robert Christian Hansen possessed that disarming ordinariness, a soft-spoken, almost shy demeanor that allowed him to navigate the bustling streets of Anchorage as an invisible man.

He might have been your neighbor, tending his garden with quiet diligence, or the polite stranger offering a murmured "good morning" as you passed. Remarkably, he was the kind of man who remembered your coffee order, a small detail that fostered a deceptive sense of trust.

But behind the comforting aroma of yeast and sugar that perpetually clung to him, behind the mundane transactions and polite inquiries, lurked a predator of chilling efficiency. A man so utterly unassuming that he moved through the world undetected, his monstrous urges masked by a veneer of normalcy. He hunted human beings with the calculated precision of a seasoned stalker, treating life as a game of pursuit and capture played out against the vast, unforgiving canvas of the Alaskan wilderness. And for years, he played this deadly game with impunity, leaving a trail of terror that would forever stain the rugged beauty of the Last Frontier.

His given name, Robert Christian Hansen, would likely have faded into the anonymity of everyday encounters. The moniker that would forever be etched in the grim annals of true crime, the title that sent a shiver down the spine of a state that prided itself on its independent spirit, was far more visceral, far more telling: The Butcher Baker.

The genesis of such profound darkness is rarely simple, often a tangled web of formative experiences and latent predispositions. For Robert Hansen, born in the quiet town of Estherville, Iowa, in 1939, the early chapters of his life were painted in shades of gray, punctuated by the harsh pronouncements of a domineering father and the stifling atmosphere of a joyless household. Young Robert was a study in social awkwardness. Plagued by shyness and a stammer that twisted his words into objects of ridicule, he became an easy target for the casual cruelty

of childhood. His face, often marred by severe acne, was another visible marker that set him apart and invited further scorn. The laughter of other children, sharp and dismissive, was a constant torment. Girls, the object of his burgeoning adolescent desires, either ignored his existence entirely or, worse, subjected him to public humiliation. These early wounds, the sting of rejection and ridicule, festered within him, creating deep scars that time would never fully erase. He carried these hurts into adulthood, a simmering resentment that would eventually find a horrifying outlet.

As adolescence yielded to young adulthood, a significant obsession began to take root in Hansen's psyche: hunting. The act of wielding a rifle, the precise mechanics of aiming and firing, offered him a sense of control that was starkly absent from his interactions with the human world.

The silence of the woods became his sanctuary, a place where the mocking laughter and judgmental gazes could not penetrate. In the vast, untamed wilderness, far from the sting of social rejection, he experienced a novel sensation: power. The ability to track, to stalk, to ultimately take a life – even that of an animal – provided a primal satisfaction, a taste of dominance that would later perversely translate into his interactions with his human victims.

By the age of twenty-one, the darker currents within Hansen began to surface in more tangible ways. In 1960, he committed an act of arson, setting fire to a school bus garage. His motive, as he later confessed, was a generalized "revenge on society," a manifestation of the simmering anger that had been brewing for years. He was apprehended, convicted, and served twenty months of a three-year prison sentence. Disturbingly, a subsequent psychological evaluation diagnosed him with an "infantile personality disorder," a term that, in retrospect, seems woefully inadequate to describe the profound pathology that lay beneath. Yet, this early brush with the law, this clear indication of disturbed behavior, failed to raise sufficient alarms, failed to divert him from the terrifying path he was already treading.

He moved on, as if the arson and the diagnosis were mere blips on his life's radar. He married, seeking perhaps a semblance of normalcy, a shield against the inner turmoil.

In 1967, he relocated to Anchorage, Alaska, a place where the vastness of the landscape seemed to swallow secrets whole. He established a bakery, a seemingly wholesome enterprise that would become the ironic backdrop to his monstrous double life. He had children, further solidifying the image of a conventional family man. And through it all, no one suspected a thing. The mask of normalcy was firmly in place, effectively concealing the predator lurking beneath.

By the decade of the 1970s, Robert Hansen had successfully cultivated a public persona as a devoted family man and a respected small business owner in the Anchorage community. He was the man who provided the morning pastries, a seemingly integral and benign part of the local landscape. But beneath this carefully constructed façade, a cauldron of resentment and rage was steadily boiling. The old wounds – the sting of rejection, the humiliation of ridicule – had not faded with time. Instead, they had festered and mutated, twisting into something far more sinister.

He began frequenting the shadowy fringes of Anchorage nightlife: the dimly lit strip clubs, the transient world of prostitutes, the smoky haze of the bars lining Fourth Avenue. He developed a pattern, a chilling routine. He would approach women, often those on the margins of society, and employ a carefully crafted charm.

He would offer them drinks, engage in seemingly innocuous conversation, sometimes pay for their company. What began as a calculated manipulation, a way to exert a measure of control, soon spiraled into something far more terrifying, a manifestation of his deep-seated need for dominance.

Within the modest confines of his Anchorage home, Hansen constructed a secret chamber, a soundproofed basement that became the physical manifestation of his dark fantasies. Inside this hidden space, he assembled the tools of his burgeoning obsession: chains, ropes, handcuffs – instruments of restraint and subjugation. It was a place designed to break the will of his victims, to reduce them to objects of his perverse control. But even this level of domination proved insufficient to satiate the growing darkness within him. His need for control, for the ultimate power over another human being, continued to escalate, pushing him towards an even more terrifying and remote arena.

The reality of Robert Hansen's crimes transcended the realm of fiction, surpassing the darkest imaginings of the most seasoned thriller writer. It was a nightmare made horrifyingly real against the backdrop of Alaska's breathtaking, yet unforgiving, wilderness. Hansen possessed a private plane, a small Piper Super Cub, a seemingly innocuous tool that became an instrument of unimaginable terror.

He would lure his victims onto the aircraft under false pretenses, promising them a ride home, a trip to a remote cabin, anything to get them airborne. Once aloft, he would navigate them far from the lights and sounds of Anchorage, deep into the desolate and empty expanse of the Alaskan backcountry. Here, miles from civilization, with no witnesses to their plight, he would reveal his true, horrifying intentions.

He would land the small plane in a remote clearing, miles from any sign of human habitation. Then, in a twisted perversion of his hunting obsession, he would release his terrified victims into the dense woods, giving them a short head start. And then he would hunt them. Armed with a rifle and drawing upon the skills honed as a big-game hunter, Hansen stalked these defenseless women as if they were animals. Some, in their desperate fight for survival, begged for their lives, their pleas swallowed by the vast silence of the wilderness. Others fought back with a primal ferocity, their resistance ultimately futile against a man armed and driven by a chilling, predatory intent. Most never stood a chance against his knowledge of the terrain, his weaponry, and his utter lack of remorse. When his gruesome hunt was complete, he would bury their remains in shallow graves scattered across the tundra, sometimes meticulously marking the locations on an aviation map – a macabre catalog of his kills.

Though Robert Hansen eventually confessed to the murders of seventeen women, authorities involved in the investigation, including myself, firmly believe that the true number of his victims may well exceed twenty. The vastness of the Alaskan wilderness, the remoteness of his hunting grounds, and the transient nature of many of his targets made a precise accounting nearly impossible. Among his known victims were Sherry Morrow, Paula Goulding, and Joanna Messina, their lives tragically cut short and their remains eventually discovered. And then there was Eklutna Annie, his first known victim, discovered near Eklutna Lake, and to this day, still unidentified, a haunting reminder of the lives Hansen stole and the identities he erased. The majority of Hansen's victims were women working on the fringes of society – sex workers, exotic dancers – individuals he likely believed would not be missed, their disappearances easily dismissed or overlooked.

But in his callous disregard for human life, he underestimated one of them.

In 1983, Robert Hansen made a crucial error, a miscalculation that would ultimately lead to the unraveling of his carefully constructed double life. He picked up a seventeen-year-old girl named Cindy Paulson. Unlike many of his previous victims, Cindy was not a dancer or a prostitute.

She was, quite simply, a survivor. A fighter. Hansen assaulted Cindy, subjecting her to the familiar ritual of chains and confinement in his soundproofed basement. He chillingly informed her that she was going to "help him out at the cabin," a thinly veiled euphemism for the horrific fate he had planned. But when Hansen momentarily turned his back, Cindy seized a fleeting opportunity. Despite being shackled and bleeding, she managed to escape his clutches, fleeing barefoot into the cold Anchorage street, her desperate cries for help cutting through the night air.

Initially, the authorities were hesitant to believe her harrowing tale. The idea that the unassuming baker was a brutal predator seemed too outlandish, too far removed from the ordinary fabric of their community. But one Alaska State Trooper, a seasoned investigator named Glenn Flothe, saw the genuine terror in Cindy's eyes and recognized the chilling consistency in her fragmented account. He believed her. An intensive investigation began, fueled by Flothe's unwavering conviction. It was a painstaking process, requiring time, patience, and the crucial acquisition of a search warrant for Hansen's seemingly ordinary residence. Eventually, the carefully constructed walls of Hansen's deception began to crumble. Inside his home, investigators unearthed a trove of damning evidence: jewelry identified as belonging to missing women, his infamous aviation map marked with the chilling "X"s indicating grave sites, a collection of weapons including the rifle linked to the murders of Morrow and Goulding, and disturbing photographs of his victims.

The evidence was irrefutable. Robert Christian Hansen, the soft-spoken baker, was arrested. Faced with the overwhelming weight of the findings, he confessed to his horrific crimes, finally revealing the monstrous truth that lay hidden beneath the baker's apron. The public, once oblivious, was confronted with the chilling reality of the predator who had walked among them for years, his unassuming facade a mask for unimaginable brutality.

To avoid the possibility of the death penalty in Alaska, Robert Hansen entered a plea deal. In 1984, he pleaded guilty to four murders but confessed to many more, providing chilling details of his hunting expeditions and the identities of some of his victims. He was ultimately sentenced to a staggering 461 years in prison, with no possibility of parole, a sentence that effectively ensured he would spend the remainder of his days behind bars. He spent the final decades of his life incarcerated at the Spring Creek Correctional Center in Seward, Alaska, the same town where the remains of Joanna Messina had been discovered. When he died in August 2014, at the age of seventy-five, his passing was met with a profound silence. There were no mourners to grieve his loss, no public memorials to mark his passing. The world simply acknowledged the end of a dark chapter.

Looking back at the Robert Hansen case, decades removed from the active investigation, a profound sense of melancholy still lingers. My thoughts often drift to the women whose stories remain incomplete, whose identities were stolen along with their lives. Hansen's crimes extended far beyond the act of murder; he systematically erased connections, leaving behind a legacy of unanswered questions and enduring pain. The true tragedy lies in the families who continue to live with the agonizing uncertainty of not knowing, their loved ones vanished without a trace, forever haunted by the unknown, never realizing that the man who might have served them coffee or sold them a loaf of bread held the key to their disappearance. The case of the Butcher Baker serves as a chilling and stark reminder that evil can often wear the most unassuming of masks, a terrifying truth that echoes through the vast and seemingly indifferent wilderness of Alaska.

- D. Boone Wilder

Chapter 3: The Face of Evil

The Joshua Wade Story

AI Generated Image of Joshua Wade

Charismatic. The word clung to Joshua Wade like a deceptive second skin. Smart, some conceded, even charming in a disarming, almost boyish way that could lull the wary into a dangerous complacency. He possessed an easy smile, a calm and steady voice that could weave a false sense of security around those who encountered him.

He knew how to project an image of affability, a surface-level pleasantness that belied the darkness festering within.

But behind that carefully constructed façade, behind the engaging grin and the soothing cadence, lurked something primal, something feral and inherently predatory. His eyes, so frequently described as calm and calculating, held a chilling stillness, watching those around him with the detached focus of a hawk circling its unsuspecting prey. In the vast, often isolating quiet of Alaska's frozen landscape, Joshua Wade didn't just hide; he thrived in the shadows, his true nature masked by the very ordinariness he so skillfully projected.

And he killed.

Anchorage, 2000 – The Beginning

The name Della Brown resonated within the tougher, more overlooked corners of Anchorage. A thirty-three-year-old Alaska Native woman, Della had navigated the treacherous currents of addiction and homelessness, yet her spirit, by all accounts, remained remarkably resilient. She was known for her unexpected kindness, her quick wit that could cut through tension, and a fearless outspokenness that endeared her to some and perhaps unsettled others. On the second day of September in the year 2000, Della's vibrant voice was brutally silenced.

Her lifeless body was discovered unceremoniously stuffed into a dilapidated shed in the Spenard area, a district known for its transient population and a persistent undercurrent of desperation. The manner of her death was savage, indicative of a rage so potent it left a visceral imprint on the scene. Her skull had been crushed, the force of the blows shattering bone and extinguishing life.

Investigators pieced together a grim narrative: Della had likely been assaulted before being bludgeoned to death with a heavy rock, the shed floor slick with the horrifying testament to her final moments – the dark, congealed stains a stark contrast to the weathered wood.

Joshua Wade's name surfaced quickly in the nascent stages of the investigation. He was a mere twenty years old, yet already a known menace within the local criminal landscape, his rap sheet a burgeoning testament to his violent tendencies. Disturbingly, Wade's own circle of acquaintances provided chilling leads, recounting how he had brazenly bragged about Della's murder, even going so far as to chillingly reenact the brutal way he had bashed in her skull. Some of these disturbing pronouncements were even captured on audio recordings, raw and unsettling evidence of a mind steeped in violence. On the surface, the case appeared to be open-and-shut, a clear path to justice for Della Brown.

But the wheels of justice, as they sometimes do, veered in an unexpected and deeply frustrating direction. Joshua Wade was ultimately brought to trial, not for the brutal murder of Della Brown, but for the comparatively minor charge of criminal mischief – for the damage inflicted upon the shed where her broken body was found. The murder charge, the very heart of the crime, was inexplicably dropped. A confluence of factors contributed to this devastating outcome. A perceived lack of definitive physical evidence directly linking Wade to the murder weapon, the challenges of relying on witnesses from a marginalized community whose testimonies were deemed "unreliable" by some, and a savvy defense that successfully painted Wade as just another misguided young punk – all coalesced to seal Della Brown's fate. Joshua Wade walked free, leaving behind a community stunned by the apparent injustice. Della Brown's life, and her violent death, were reduced to a mere footnote in the local crime blotter, a tragic casualty of a system that seemed to falter when the victim was deemed less worthy of its full attention.

The One That Couldn't Be Ignored – Mindy Schloss

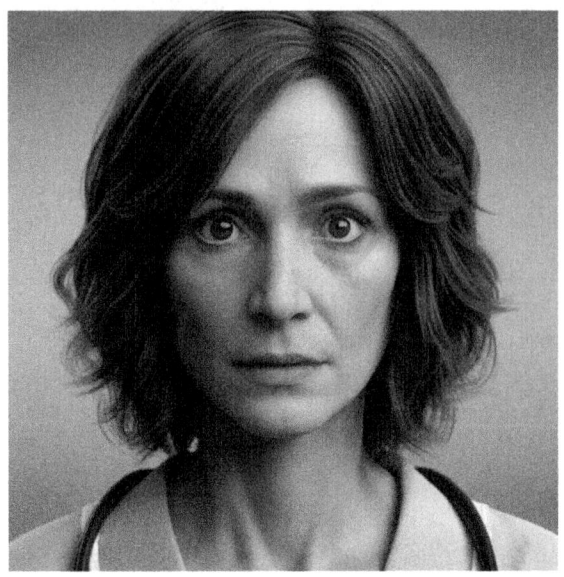

AI Generated Image of Mindy Schloss

Seven years passed, a span of time during which Joshua Wade continued to walk among the living, the ghost of Della Brown perhaps a silent companion to his escalating darkness. Then, in the late summer of 2007, another life intersected with his, a life that would ultimately ignite the long-dormant embers of justice.

Dr. Mindy Schloss was a respected and dedicated nurse practitioner, a woman known for her compassionate care and calming presence. She had chosen to relocate to Anchorage from the Lower 48, drawn by the promise of a peaceful existence amidst the rugged beauty of the Last Frontier. Mindy had poured her heart into her work, her quiet dedication earning her the respect and affection of her patients and colleagues.

When Mindy inexplicably failed to show up for work in late August of 2007, a wave of alarm rippled through her close circle of friends. A missing person report was quickly filed, and the ensuing police investigation soon uncovered disturbing clues. Mindy's car was found abandoned, bearing the chilling evidence of bloodstains within the vehicle, the crimson smears stark against the upholstery. Surveillance footage surfaced, capturing a man using Mindy's ATM card – a man later positively identified as Joshua Wade.

Within days, the authorities were closing in on him. Wade was apprehended and initially charged with car theft and fraud, while investigators frantically worked against the clock to locate Mindy, the growing fear palpable in the sterile environment of the precinct. On September 13, 2007, the worst fears were realized. Mindy Schloss's lifeless body was discovered in a remote, wooded area, a stark echo of the wilderness that had claimed Della Brown years before. The manner of her death was cold and calculated: a single gunshot wound to the head, an execution-style killing that spoke volumes about the callousness of her murderer. Mindy Schloss was fifty-two years old, her life, like Della Brown's, cut short by the violent hand of Joshua Wade.

This time, however, Wade's practiced charm and manipulative rhetoric would prove insufficient. The evidence against him was overwhelming, a damning tapestry woven from ballistics analysis matching the bullet to Wade's firearm, meticulous phone records placing him at key locations, and the irrefutable images captured on security footage. Joshua Wade was finally charged with the first-degree murder of Mindy Schloss. He ultimately pleaded guilty, perhaps recognizing the futility of further denial in the face of such compelling evidence.

The Truth Comes Too Late

It wasn't until 2010, three years after his guilty plea and subsequent sentencing to life in prison without the possibility of parole for the murder of Mindy Schloss, that the dam of Joshua Wade's carefully guarded secrets finally began to crack. In a sickening and calculated confession, Wade admitted to the long-unsolved 2000 murder of Della Brown, the crime for which he had so brazenly evaded justice years earlier. But his revelations didn't end there. He chillingly claimed to have murdered a total of five people, including Schloss and Brown. The identities of the other alleged victims remained shrouded in a disturbing ambiguity – locations vague, names unspoken, lost perhaps forever to the Alaskan wilderness.

This unsettling confession was offered as part of a bizarre plea deal aimed at avoiding the death penalty in federal court, a final, manipulative attempt to control his narrative and cheat the ultimate consequence. He delivered these chilling admissions with a smirk, a disturbing display of callousness that sent a cold wave through those who listened. Based on Wade's own admissions and the lingering questions surrounding other unsolved disappearances during his reign of terror, authorities came to a grim conclusion: Joshua Wade may have been Alaska's most overlooked and underestimated serial killer, his true body count a haunting unknown.

Reflections from the Badge

When I first delved into the details of Della Brown's case, a wave of profound anger washed over me. Not just at the blatant injustice that had allowed Joshua Wade to walk free after such a brutal crime, but because I've witnessed firsthand the subtle, yet pervasive, ways in which the system can sometimes turn a blind eye when the victim doesn't fit a certain profile – when they are not middle-class, white, or perceived as "respectable." Della Brown deserved justice in 2000. The evidence, though perhaps not pristine, was there. The chilling boasts, the audio recordings… it should have been enough to keep him off the streets.

Instead, we lost seven more years, seven years during which a predator continued to walk free, and tragically, at least one more innocent life – that of Mindy Schloss – was brutally extinguished. This loss weighs heavily. It speaks to a failure, not just within the judicial process, but within societal perceptions, a tendency to devalue certain lives and dismiss the cries for help from the marginalized. We didn't listen closely enough to the whispers, to the concerns raised by those who knew Della. We allowed Wade's superficial charm and clever manipulation to outweigh the hard, brutal truth of his actions. As a law enforcement officer, this kind of failure eats at you, a constant reminder of the lives that might have been saved, the suffering that could have been prevented. As a man, it haunts you, the image of Della Brown's broken body a stark testament to the consequences of indifference. Evil doesn't always manifest as a monstrous figure lurking in the shadows. Sometimes, it wears a disarming smile, speaks with a calm voice, and tells you exactly what you want to hear. And in Alaska, for far too long, Joshua Wade's deceptive facade was believed.

Final Reflection by Investigator Boone Wilder

The enduring legacy of Joshua Wade's heinous crimes serves as a chilling and vital reminder of the insidious ways in which evil can conceal itself in plain sight. It is not always the grotesque figure lurking in the darkness that poses the greatest threat; often, it is the seemingly charming, manipulative personality that can deceive even those trained to recognize danger.

Wade's disturbing ability to manipulate the system, to evade justice for years, and to continue his deadly path reflects a profound failure not only within the judicial process but also within our societal perceptions of what a killer truly looks like.

We must remember Della Brown and Mindy Schloss not merely as statistics or headlines, but as vibrant human beings whose lives were tragically cut short. They serve as stark reminders of the profound human cost of such failures. Justice must not only be swift but also thorough and equitable, blind to societal biases. Assumptions based on superficial appearances must never dictate the course of an investigation or the value we place on a human life. As I reflect on this deeply troubling case, I am constantly reminded that our duty as law enforcement officers extends beyond simply following the presented evidence. It demands that we critically question our own biases, actively challenge complacency, and amplify the voices of the vulnerable. Joshua Wade was a predator who operated in plain sight, but he thrived for years because the system, and perhaps society itself, underestimated him. That is a painful lesson we must never, ever forget.

- D. Boone Wilder

Chapter 4: The Cold Calculations of Isreal Keyes

The Isreal Keyes Story

AI Generated Image of Isreal Keyes

A true nomadic predator, Keyes moved across the vast expanse of the United States like a phantom, his presence leaving barely a ripple in the waters of everyday life. His chilling methodology involved planting caches of deadly supplies – his self-described "kill kits" – years in advance. These sinister time capsules lay dormant in remote, carefully selected locations, buried beneath the earth, awaiting his command.

He would return to these hidden arsenals years later, drawn by an internal, unknowable trigger, to commit his unspeakable acts, leaving behind a landscape scrubbed clean of his presence, offering no warning, no discernible pattern for law enforcement to decipher. For the myriad local and federal agencies tasked with piecing together the fragments of his crimes, it wasn't simply a matter of playing catch-up in the aftermath of a murder. They were often operating in complete darkness, unaware that a deadly game was even being played, the pieces of a horrific puzzle scattered across state lines, the rules dictated by a mind operating on a terrifyingly unique and unfathomable plane. For years, the rugged, isolated beauty of Alaska, a land that often swallowed secrets whole, served as his unsuspecting home base, the seemingly innocuous launching point for his chilling and far-reaching expeditions into darkness.

Early Life and Disturbing Signs

Born amidst the stark, unforgiving landscapes of Utah and raised within the insular confines of rural Washington, Israel Keyes emerged from an isolated, fundamentalist upbringing. Homeschooling shielded him from the influences of mainstream society, fostering a worldview shaped by the strict tenets of his family's beliefs. A heavy emphasis on self-sufficiency instilled in him a deep proficiency with firearms and the practical skills required to live off the land from a young age.

This upbringing, while perhaps intended to cultivate independence and resilience, inadvertently nurtured a profound sense of self-reliance that bordered on detachment, a chilling disconnect from the common threads of human empathy.

In the late 1990s and early 2000s, Keyes drifted through a series of transient construction jobs, the nomadic nature of his work mirroring a deep-seated internal restlessness. He fathered a child, a brief and ultimately unsuccessful foray into a semblance of a conventional domestic life, before eventually settling into the anonymity of Anchorage, Alaska. There, he established a small contracting business, Keyes Construction.

Clients who hired him described him in unremarkable terms: polite, professional, efficient – the kind of person who blended seamlessly into the background noise of everyday life, leaving no lasting impression. But beneath this carefully constructed veneer of normalcy, a darker, more sinister existence quietly took root.

Keyes harbored a chilling and growing fascination with the shadows. He developed a disturbing habit of stalking individuals in the dead of night, the thrill of remaining unseen, the potent allure of potential violence stirring within. He broke into homes, not necessarily driven by the need to steal, but for "practice" – a perverse rehearsal for the ultimate act of intrusion and violation. And in the silent, solitary confines of his thoughts, he meticulously constructed elaborate and increasingly violent fantasies of murder, each scenario a deliberate step further down a path of unimaginable brutality.

The Methodical Killer

Israel Keyes elevated the concept of premeditation to a level that left even the most seasoned FBI profilers reeling. Years before he even selected his victims, he would meticulously plan and execute the burial of plastic buckets in remote, carefully chosen locations scattered across the vast expanse of the country. These weren't mere hiding places; they were his chilling "kill kits," containing a carefully curated array of deadly supplies: weapons, substantial amounts of cash, restraints, and cleaning supplies designed to meticulously erase every trace of his presence. He would then lie dormant, sometimes for years, until an internal, unknowable trigger compelled him to return to these pre-positioned arsenals to commit his unspeakable acts of violence.

He deliberately and meticulously avoided committing murders in or near his Anchorage home, maintaining a calculated and crucial separation between his seemingly ordinary everyday life and his horrific double existence. He never targeted individuals he knew, consciously eliminating any personal connection that might provide a discernible link for investigators. His motivation wasn't rooted in hatred, revenge, or even financial gain; it was a far more chilling and unsettling impulse – a cold, insatiable need for absolute control, a perverse desire to exert the ultimate power over another human being's life and death, simply because he could.

The Final Mistake: Samantha Koenig

AI Generated Image of Samantha Koenig

Yet, in a cruel and ironic twist of fate, it was Anchorage, the very place he so carefully avoided as a hunting ground, that ultimately led to his undoing in the early months of 2012. On the first day of February, eighteen-year-old Samantha Koenig was working her routine shift at a small, brightly lit coffee kiosk nestled in the bustling midtown area of Anchorage. The grainy black and white surveillance footage captured what appeared to be a seemingly ordinary late-night encounter: a man approaching her window, a brief exchange of words, the sudden, unsettling glint of a handgun.

Samantha, likely gripped by terror but displaying a heartbreaking compliance, turned off the kiosk lights and walked out into the cold, unforgiving Alaskan night with him.

Her family's desperate and increasingly frantic pleas for her safe return echoed through the city, a tight-knit community gripped by a growing sense of fear and unease. What no one in the terrified community knew, what remained a horrifying secret held solely within the cold, calculating mind of Israel Keyes, was that Samantha Koenig was already dead. In a chilling display of calculated cruelty and a desire to further torment her loved ones, Keyes kept her lifeless body in a shed located behind his unassuming Anchorage home. He even went so far as to pose her for a ransom photograph, sewing her eyes open with fishing line to create the grotesque illusion that she was still alive, a final, heartless act of deception. He then dismembered her remains and callously disposed of them in the frigid, murky waters of Matanuska Lake, attempting to erase her existence as thoroughly as he had erased her life.

The Capture and Confession

Keyes's fatal flaw, the chink in his otherwise meticulously crafted armor of deception, proved to be a manifestation of his own arrogance and a careless disregard for the increasingly sophisticated tools of modern law enforcement.

He began using Samantha's debit card on a brazen cross-country road trip in the weeks following her abduction and murder, withdrawing relatively small amounts of cash from ATMs in Arizona, New Mexico, and Texas. Each transaction, however, seemingly insignificant, left a digital breadcrumb trail, a silent witness to his movements. Law enforcement agencies, working tirelessly and collaboratively across state lines, meticulously followed this electronic trail, eventually tracking him down and apprehending him in the quiet town of Lufkin, Texas.

Once in custody, Keyes began to speak, but only on his own terms, his chillingly detached demeanor unwavering. He readily admitted to the abduction and murder of Samantha Koenig, but this confession was merely the visible tip of a terrifying and deeply submerged iceberg. He went on to confess to at least seven other murders, including the baffling and long-unsolved disappearance of Bill and Lorraine Currier from Essex, Vermont.

His recounts of these horrific acts were delivered with a clinical detachment, devoid of remorse or any discernible emotion, as if he were recounting the details of a mundane task. In December of 2012, while still incarcerated and facing the full weight of the crimes he had confessed to, Israel Keyes took his own life, severing the thread of his dark narrative and leaving behind a chilling void of countless unanswered questions.

He took his secrets to the grave, the true number of his victims remaining a haunting and disturbing subject of speculation for investigators and the families of the missing. The locations of his buried kill kits, potential evidence of other unspeakable acts, may forever remain hidden beneath the vast American landscape.

Reflections from the Badge

Reflecting on the profoundly disturbing case of Israel Keyes, it is not solely the known victims who haunt the collective consciousness. It is the vast expanse of the unknown, the chilling specter of the unanswered questions, the potential for buried "kill kits" that may never be unearthed, the families who may forever remain in the agonizing limbo of not knowing the fate of their missing loved ones. Keyes didn't simply kill; he manipulated, controlled, and deceived with a chilling efficiency that defied comprehension. He operated like a phantom, his presence leaving only faint whispers and lingering fear in his wake.

For law enforcement, Israel Keyes represents the ultimate nightmare: a predator who hunted without discernible pattern or geographic limitation, leaving behind no personal motive, operating on a level of meticulous planning and calculated detachment that defied conventional criminal profiling.

As I reflect on this case, I am reminded that the most dangerous monsters are not always the ones who announce their arrival with overt aggression. Sometimes, it is the quiet ones, the individuals who master the art of blending into the ordinary, who possess the chilling ability to hide their monstrous nature in plain sight, who ultimately leave the deepest and most enduring scars on the fabric of our society. The case of Israel Keyes remains a grim and unsettling reminder that profound evil can often wear the most unassuming of faces, and that the relentless pursuit of justice, the unwavering commitment to uncovering the truth, must never waver – even when confronted by a darkness that seems insurmountable and a silence that may never be fully broken.

- D. Boone Wilder

Chapter 5: The Investor Murders

Fire, Silence, and the Sea

September 5th, 1982. The bustling harbor of Craig, Alaska—a rugged fishing town nestled on Prince of Wales Island— pulsed with the raw energy of the end of the salmon season. Fishing boats, large and small, maneuvered through the crowded channels, their crews weary but triumphant after months battling the unpredictable Alaskan waters, eager to unload their final hauls. Amidst this flurry of activity, the *Investor*, a sturdy fifty-eight-foot salmon seiner, slipped quietly into its mooring, an unassuming vessel returning from a successful season. Onboard were eight souls: the boat's owner, Mark Coulthurst, a respected figure in the close-knit fishing community; his pregnant wife, Irene, anticipating the joys of motherhood once more; their two young children, eight-year-old Kimberly and five-year-old John, their innocent laughter soon to echo on the docks; and four hardworking deckhands, their faces etched with the lines of the sea. Eight lives, brimming with the promise of reunion and rest, utterly unaware of the unimaginable darkness that lay in wait.

AI Generated Image of The Investor on Fire

Three days later, on the morning of September 8th, the *Investor* was discovered adrift near the desolate shores of Fish Egg Island, a grim spectacle against the serene backdrop of the Alaskan waters. Flames, angry and voracious, engulfed the vessel, spewing thick, acrid black smoke that billowed into the clear sky, a stark and horrifying contrast to the tranquil blue of the surrounding sea. Locals watched in stunned silence as the familiar silhouette of the fishing boat was consumed by the relentless fire, a premonition of disaster sinking deep in their hearts.

By the time the first responders managed to board the scorched and listing remains of the *Investor*, the heat still radiating from the charred hull, it was tragically too late. Inside the gutted vessel lay the incinerated bodies of Mark, Irene, Kimberly, and John, their final moments undoubtedly filled with terror. Alongside them were the barely recognizable remains of the four deckhands, their identities almost completely erased by the intense heat. Some bodies were so thoroughly burned, so reduced to ash and bone fragments, that they were never fully recovered from the unforgiving sea. The initial investigation quickly confirmed the horrifying truth: this was no accident, no tragic mechanical failure. The presence of unmistakable gunshot wounds etched into the remains made it chillingly clear – this was a calculated and brutal massacre.

A single, agonizing question hung heavy in the stunned atmosphere of Craig: who could have committed such an atrocity? Why target a seemingly upstanding family and their hardworking crew, individuals who were generally respected and well-liked within the close-knit fishing community? As the investigation lurched into motion, casting a wide net across the small town and its surrounding areas, a potential suspect began to emerge from the periphery.

Witnesses, their memories sharpened by the horror of the event, recalled seeing a stranger lingering around the docks in the days leading up to the tragedy – a man who didn't quite fit the familiar faces of the local fishermen. He had been observed engaging in brief conversations with the crew of the *Investor*, and some even claimed to have seen him board the vessel before it cast off for its final, ill-fated journey. Based on these fragmented recollections, the police released a composite sketch, a ghostly image of a man with an unsettlingly unremarkable face. But despite the distribution of the sketch and the initial flurry of leads, concrete answers remained frustratingly sparse.

Eventually, the investigative focus narrowed on John Kenneth Peel, a former deckhand who had worked for Mark Coulthurst during the previous fishing season. Peel had a reputation for being a bit of a loner, an individual who kept to himself and didn't readily engage with the social fabric of the town. While nothing in his past suggested a propensity for extreme violence, he nonetheless fit the general descriptions provided by some of the witnesses. Crucially, it was also known that Peel had been in Craig around the time of the murders, a fact that placed him squarely within the timeline of the horrific events.

Based on this circumstantial web of suspicion, John Kenneth Peel was arrested and charged with eight counts of murder, a staggering accusation that sent shockwaves through the state of Alaska, bracing it for a trial that would become the longest and most expensive in its history.

The first trial commenced in 1986, a grueling six-month legal marathon that gripped the attention of the entire state. For what seemed like an eternity, the prosecution meticulously presented its case, attempting to paint John Kenneth Peel as a disgruntled former employee harboring a deep-seated grudge against Mark Coulthurst, a resentment that had allegedly festered and finally erupted in a paroxysm of unimaginable violence. Yet, despite the lengthy presentation and the emotional weight of the accusations, the evidence remained largely circumstantial at best. The prosecution could produce no murder weapon definitively linked to Peel, no confession extracted from his tightly sealed lips, and no direct forensic evidence unequivocally connecting him to the scene of the crime or the victims. After weeks of intense deliberation, the jury remained hopelessly deadlocked, unable to reach the unanimous verdict required for a conviction. A mistrial was declared, leaving the families of the victims and the community of Craig reeling with disappointment and a renewed sense of agonizing uncertainty.

Two years later, in 1988, the state of Alaska decided to retry John Kenneth Peel, a testament to their unwavering belief in his guilt and their commitment to seeking justice for the eight lost souls. This time, however, the defense mounted a more effective and strategic challenge, meticulously dissecting the prosecution's reliance on circumstantial evidence. They skillfully cast doubt on the credibility of the eyewitness accounts, highlighting inconsistencies and the passage of time, and forcefully emphasized the glaring absence of concrete physical proof linking Peel to the murders. After another protracted and emotionally draining trial, the jury once again wrestled with the ambiguous evidence. Ultimately, they returned a verdict that sent a collective gasp of disbelief and outrage through the community of Craig and the state of Alaska: John Kenneth Peel was acquitted of all eight counts of murder. In a final, bitter twist, Peel later sued the state for wrongful prosecution, eventually receiving a substantial settlement of $900,000, a financial compensation that felt like a profound insult to the memory of the victims and a stark reminder of the justice that had eluded them.

The verdict left the families of Mark, Irene, Kimberly, John, and the four deckhands feeling utterly hollow and profoundly frustrated, the promise of justice dissolving into the cold reality of an unsolved crime.

To this day, no one else has ever been charged in connection with the horrific *Investor* murders. The case remains officially unsolved, a haunting and enduring mystery that continues to cast a long shadow over the small fishing town of Craig and the broader Alaskan community. For those in law enforcement who poured their hearts and souls into the investigation, the frustration remains palpable, a gnawing sense of unfinished business that lingers like the smell of smoke on a cold morning.

Former Chief Boone Wilder, reflecting on the enduring tragedy, emphasizes the profound impact of the calculated destruction and the agonizing lack of closure on all who knew and loved the victims. "Eight people boarded the *Investor* that September day," Wilder states, his voice heavy with the weight of memory, "but none of them ever came home. Somewhere out there, the killer, or killers, may have simply walked away – quiet, free, and perhaps even forgotten by the wider world, but never by those who were left behind. The fire may have been extinguished, but the silence that followed still screams in the hearts of those who remember."

The *Investor* Murders stand as a chilling and stark reminder that not all cases find resolution, that sometimes evil can lurk behind seemingly familiar faces and walk away unscathed, leaving a legacy of unanswered questions and enduring pain.

The silence surrounding the brutal murders continues to echo through the decades, a cold case that still burns with a quiet intensity in the collective memory of Alaska's tight-knit fishing community, a wound that refuses to fully heal beneath the vast and indifferent Alaskan sky.

- D. Boone Wilder

Chapter 6: Murder On Snapchat

The Brian Smith Murders

It began not with a frantic 911 call, not with the chilling discovery of a body in a desolate alley, but with a digital whisper, a fleeting glimpse into a world of unimaginable horror. A scream, raw and visceral, momentarily pierced the silence. Then, the crackle of static, the electronic ghost of a dying connection. And finally, a voice, chillingly calm and measured: "Just…just take a breath." What followed this unsettling prelude was a haunting, fragmented video, a digital snapshot of a nightmare that no one was ever intended to witness.

But it was seen. Accidentally broadcast across the ephemeral landscape of social media, it landed on the screen of a horrified friend, who, recognizing the terror unfolding, acted swiftly, alerting the authorities. That accidental transmission, that unintended window into a brutal reality, cracked open a murder case so horrific in its cruelty, so surreal in its unfolding, that it not only dominated national headlines but left even the most seasoned investigators, those hardened by years of confronting human depravity, momentarily speechless.

The killer was not some shadowy drifter who materialized from the Alaskan wilderness. He wasn't a long-sought-after mystery, a phantom flitting through the periphery of society. He was hiding in plain sight, a seemingly assimilated immigrant who had diligently built a life in the unassuming landscape of Anchorage, Alaska. And the victim was a young Alaska Native woman, one of society's often overlooked and marginalized, desperately trying to navigate a world that had long turned its back on her, a world where her struggles often went unnoticed, her voice unheard.

The Snapchat Confession

In the early days of September 2019, the Anchorage Police Department received an unusual and deeply disturbing tip, a digital breadcrumb leading into the abyss. A woman, her voice trembling with shock and disbelief, reported witnessing a horrific video posted to the ephemeral platform of Snapchat. The short, fleeting clip showed a man engaged in a brutal assault on a visibly distressed Alaska Native woman. The woman in the video appeared terrified, her face bloodied and bruised, a stark testament to the violence she had endured. The man, in chilling contrast, remained eerily calm and composed, his demeanor a mask of cold detachment. This was no prank, no elaborate digital hoax designed to shock and disturb. This was real. Unflinchingly, horrifyingly real.

The victim in the Snapchat video was later identified as Kathleen Henry, a thirty-year-old Alaska Native woman whose life had been marked by the struggles of addiction and homelessness, challenges that often leave individuals vulnerable and unseen. Her path had been undeniably difficult, fraught with obstacles and hardships. But regardless of her struggles, regardless of the societal neglect she may have faced, no one, absolutely no one, deserves the brutal and dehumanizing fate that befell Kathleen Henry

AI Generated Image of Kathleen Henry

In the fragmented audio of the Snapchat video, the man's voice could be heard, laced with a chilling mockery as he berated his victim.

At one point, he callously ordered her to "calm down," a cruel and ironic demand in the face of the terror she was experiencing. In another haunting snippet, Kathleen's voice, weak and filled with mortal fear, could be heard pleading, "I don't want to die." Her desperate plea went unanswered. She did.

Who Was Brian Smith?

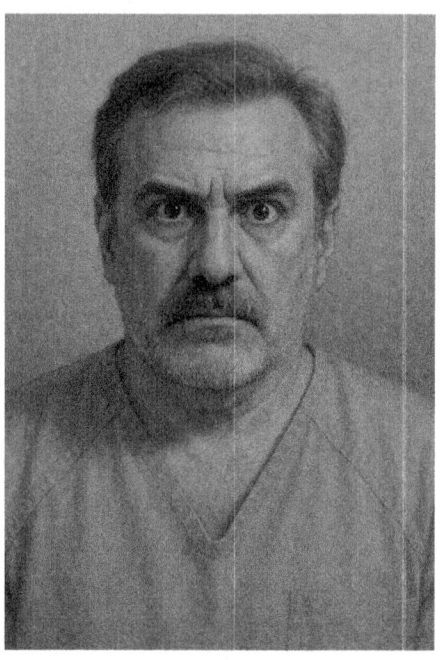

AI Generated Image of Brian Smith

Brian Steven Smith was a forty-eight-year-old immigrant from South Africa who had married an American woman and, on the surface, had meticulously constructed a seemingly stable and unremarkable life in the sprawling landscape of Alaska. He held down odd jobs, traveled both within and outside the state, and readily smiled for photographs, projecting an image of normalcy and contentment. Nothing in his outward presentation raised any immediate red flags, no obvious indicators of the darkness that festered within. But behind the closed doors of his Anchorage residence, something profoundly sinister was quietly brewing, a malignant growth of depravity that would eventually erupt into unimaginable violence.

When investigators, armed with the crucial Snapchat video, meticulously tracked the associated IP address and painstakingly identified the man captured in the horrifying clip, their focus narrowed with chilling precision on Brian Steven Smith. What they discovered in the subsequent investigation went far beyond their initial, grim expectations. In his unassuming Anchorage home – and later, with the aid of digital forensics, on his personal cell phone – police uncovered a trove of additional videos and dozens upon dozens of disturbing photographs documenting what could only be described as a macabre murder trophy collection. These digital files were not mere snapshots of violence; they were a chilling catalog of cruelty, a testament to a mind that reveled in the suffering of others.

One particularly disturbing video depicted Smith actively choking Kathleen Henry, his face contorted not in anger, but in what appeared to be a perverse form of laughter, a chilling soundtrack to her final moments. Another harrowing video revealed a second woman, later identified as thirty-year-old Veronica Abouchuk, who had been missing for over a year, her disappearance a silent tragedy that had barely registered in the wider consciousness. Veronica Abouchuk was already deceased when law enforcement viewed the horrifying footage, another victim claimed by the darkness that had lurked undetected within Brian Smith.

AI Generated Image of Veronica Abouchuk

The Arrest and the Evidence

Brian Steven Smith was apprehended at Ted Stevens Anchorage International Airport on October 8, 2019, as he returned from an out-of-state trip, his seemingly ordinary arrival masking the monstrous reality of his recent actions. His reaction upon being confronted by law enforcement was one of feigned surprise, a carefully constructed mask of innocence. He vehemently denied any involvement in the horrific events, attempting to deflect suspicion and maintain the facade of the ordinary man he had so diligently cultivated. But the digital evidence, the silent witnesses captured on his own devices, proved to be overwhelming and irrefutable. Two deceased women. Two horrifying videos documenting their final moments. One cold-blooded killer whose carefully constructed facade had finally shattered.

Police swiftly charged him with two counts of first-degree murder, along with charges of tampering with evidence and misconduct involving a corpse, reflecting the callous and dehumanizing way he had treated his victims. As the investigation continued to unfold, the initial charges would only grow in severity and scope as more damning evidence surfaced from the digital realm.

The police uncovered a deeply disturbing pattern in Smith's digital footprint, including repeated and explicit searches for violent pornography, methods of disposing of human bodies, and techniques for manipulating digital recordings, revealing a chilling premeditation and a disturbing fascination with the darkest aspects of human behavior.

The Digital Age of Evil

The case of Brian Smith was not solved through the traditional avenues of detective work. There was no frantic 911 call placed by a witness to the unfolding horror. No chance encounter on the street that led to the identification of a suspect. No tell-tale fingerprints left on a discarded object at a conventional crime scene. This horrific case cracked open, the darkness illuminated, because a Snapchat story, a fleeting digital moment, had inadvertently auto-uploaded without the killer's awareness, a technological glitch that became a lifeline for justice. Kathleen Henry, in her final, desperate moments, had somehow, perhaps unknowingly, set her phone to record. That digital recording, a silent scream captured in data, uploaded just enough fragmented evidence for a horrified friend to sound the alarm, to pull back the curtain on the unimaginable evil that had claimed her life. In a twisted and tragic irony, it was Kathleen Henry's final, unintended act of resistance, her voice broadcast across the digital ether, that ultimately led to the identification and apprehension of her killer.

Reflections from the Badge

There is a distinct and unsettling quality to this case, a layer of depravity that chills even the most seasoned investigators to the bone. I have witnessed firsthand the brutal aftermath of violence, the tragic consequences of monsters who operate in the shadows, their motives often rooted in the familiar, albeit twisted, landscapes of rage or desperation. But this... this was different. This was a man who meticulously recorded his cruelty, cataloged the suffering he inflicted, and likely relived those horrific moments in the solitude of his own mind. That level of cold, calculated depravity does not simply materialize out of thin air. It speaks to a profound and deeply ingrained darkness, a chilling detachment from the fundamental value of human life.

What breaks my heart, what casts a long and somber shadow over this case, is the undeniable fact that both Kathleen Henry and Veronica Abouchuk were Indigenous women, members of a community that has historically been marginalized and underserved. And like so many before them, their disappearances barely registered beyond their immediate circles, their stories fading into the background until the cold, unblinking eye of technology captured the killer in his horrific act.

The case of Brian Smith shines a harsh and unforgiving light on a dark and persistent truth in Alaska – and far beyond its borders: Far too many Native women go missing, their disappearances often met with a shocking indifference, their stories lost in the vastness of the landscape and the complexities of societal neglect. Too few resources are dedicated to their cases, too few voices raised in outrage.

Kathleen Henry's death was undeniably horrific, a brutal and senseless act of violence. But in her final, unknowing moments, through the accidental broadcast of her terror, she helped to catch her killer. She spoke when the world had too often silenced her. And that – that is something profoundly worth remembering. Her voice, though tragically muffled in life, rang out in death. And because of it, justice, however belated, finally got a name.

- D. Boone Wilder

Chapter 7: The Betrayal of Trust

The Thomas Richard Bunday Murders

There exists a sacred and inviolable trust between the public and those who choose to wear the uniform of law enforcement, the symbol of military service. We, as guardians of the peace and defenders of our nation, are entrusted with a profound and solemn responsibility: to protect the vulnerable, to serve with unwavering integrity, and to lead by the very example of our conduct. When that fundamental trust is irrevocably shattered – when the very symbol of authority becomes a mask concealing a predator, a wolf in sheep's clothing – the damage inflicted extends far beyond the immediate acts of violence. It festers like a wound, casting long and insidious shadows of doubt and fear over the entire community, eroding the very foundations of faith and security.

That is the dark and enduring legacy of Thomas Richard Bunday in the close-knit community of Fairbanks, Alaska, during the chilling years of the early 1980s. The killer who haunted this northern town, instilling a pervasive sense of dread that clung to the very air, was not a shadowy stranger who drifted in from the vast Alaskan wilderness.

He was not an outsider, easily dismissed as someone separate from their own. He was one of their own – a U.S. Air Force Staff Sergeant stationed at the sprawling Eielson Air Force Base, a vital part of the local landscape. He was a father, a husband, a seemingly ordinary man who donned the uniform of his country each day – a potent symbol of order, dedicated service, and unwavering protection. Yet, behind that polished brass and crisp fabric, beneath the veneer of respectability, a festering darkness was quietly consuming him, a malignancy that would ultimately erupt in a series of unimaginable losses, leaving a scar on the collective soul of Fairbanks.

AI Generated Image of Thomas Richard Bunday

Fairbanks, a town intimately acquainted with the biting chill of sub-zero temperatures and the long, dark embrace of winter, faced a different kind of cold in the years 1981 and 1982 – a pervasive fear that seeped deeper than the icy winds sweeping across the seemingly endless expanse of the tundra. One by one, young women began to vanish without a trace, their sudden disappearances casting a heavy pall of anxiety and uncertainty over the tight-knit community. Marlene Peters, a vibrant twenty-year-old woman full of life and promise, simply vanished into thin air in March of 1981, leaving behind a void that her loved ones struggled to comprehend. In July of the same year, nineteen-year-old Glinda Sodemann also disappeared, her absence adding another layer of fear to the already unsettling atmosphere. August brought the particularly heartbreaking disappearance of eleven-year-old Doris Oehring, a tragic loss of innocence that shocked even the most seasoned law enforcement officers, a stark reminder of the predator's chilling reach. By the late summer months, the worst fears were realized when sixteen-year-old Wendy Wilson's lifeless body was discovered, a brutal confirmation of the darkness that stalked their streets. Then, in the early months of 1982, nineteen-year-old Malinda Williams was last seen, her fate remaining to this day a haunting and unresolved mystery, a constant source of anguish for her family and the community.

The victims shared a heartbreaking and unsettling vulnerability. They were young, female, some Alaska Native, already facing the systemic challenges and prejudices of their heritage, other runaways seeking a fragile independence, and some simply young women who found themselves in the wrong place at the wrong time, their paths tragically intersecting with a predator hiding in plain sight. Fear, a palpable and suffocating presence, gripped Fairbanks as the list of missing women grew longer, each disappearance fueling the growing sense of dread. Yet, the predator they sought was not some nameless monster lurking in the shadows, a figure easily othered and dismissed. He was someone who lived among them, a neighbor, a familiar face, a man cloaked in the perceived honor and authority of military service, his uniform a deceptive shield against suspicion.

Thomas Bunday meticulously cultivated the image of the ideal American serviceman – seemingly bright, disciplined, and driven, a man dedicated to his duty. Born in the heart of Texas in 1948, he had enlisted in the U.S. Air Force, married, and steadily risen through the ranks to the position of Staff Sergeant, a testament to his apparent commitment and competence. To his neighbors in Fairbanks, he presented as polite, quiet, and professional – a reliable and unassuming figure within the community, the kind of man who blended seamlessly into the background.

Yet, behind that composed and outwardly respectable demeanor, Bunday was silently unraveling, a storm of inner turmoil brewing beneath the surface. He grappled with a gnawing sense of guilt and a simmering rage, fueled by a troubled past marked by unresolved sexual frustration, deep-seated emotional trauma, and a volatile temper that could flare with startling and unpredictable intensity. His marriage was strained, the intimacy fractured by his internal conflicts, and his feelings toward women were tragically tainted by resentment and a distorted perception. He wore his military uniform like an impenetrable shield, a symbol of authority that effectively concealed the festering darkness within.

In 1983, Bunday's time in Alaska abruptly ended when he received a military transfer back to Texas, unknowingly removing the predator from the hunting grounds he had so chillingly exploited. But detectives in Fairbanks, diligently piecing together the scattered fragments of evidence, the unsettling coincidences and the lingering questions, began to focus their suspicions on the seemingly upstanding Staff Sergeant. His name surfaced after witnesses, their memories jogged by the growing intensity of the investigation, reported seeing his vehicle in the vicinity of at least one of the crime scenes around the time of a disappearance. During the initial questioning by authorities, Bunday remained eerily calm and collected, his responses almost too measured, his demeanor unsettlingly mechanical, devoid of any genuine emotion or concern. Then came the crucial break in the investigation – a partial confession, chilling in its cold detachment, delivered not to the Alaska authorities but to law enforcement officials in Texas.

In those chilling admissions, Bunday confessed to the murders of at least five young women in Alaska, the details he provided painting a disturbing picture of calculated violence and a profound lack of empathy. He spoke of the "thrill" he derived from his heinous acts, the overwhelming compulsions that drove him, and the terrifying randomness with which he selected his victims, their lives extinguished seemingly on a whim. There was no remorse in his carefully chosen words, no flicker of regret in his eyes – only a cold and clinical recounting of his unspeakable actions. Before the wheels of justice could fully turn, before he could be extradited back to Alaska to face the consequences of his crimes, Thomas Bunday took flight, a man running not just from the law but from the inescapable weight of his own conscience. He embarked on a desperate journey through the southern states, a predator now a fugitive, until his flight ended abruptly and tragically on March 15, 1983, when he crashed his motorcycle into an oncoming truck in Texas – a final, fatal act that bore the chilling hallmarks of suicide by speed.

No trial. No justice served in a courtroom. Just a sudden, violent death that robbed the victims' families of the closure they so desperately deserved, of the satisfaction of seeing their daughters' killer held accountable for his horrific actions. The abrupt end to Bunday's life left the community of Fairbanks not only mourning the precious lives that had been so cruelly stolen but also grappling with the bitter and unsettling reality that the monster they had feared, the predator who had haunted their town, had worn the uniform of a protector, a symbol of the very trust he had so profoundly betrayed.

Reflections from the Badge

When evil chooses to wear a uniform, it casts a dark and indelible stain upon the entire brotherhood, upon the very ideals that uniform is meant to represent. Thomas Bunday's crimes were not simply acts of murder; they were profound and deeply personal betrayals of the sacred trust placed upon those who serve. Every oath he swore to uphold, every crisp salute he rendered, every single day he donned that uniform became a calculated and chilling lie, a deceptive mask concealing the darkness within. What makes this case so deeply disturbing, so profoundly unsettling, is the acute sense of betrayal that permeates every aspect of it.

These young women, some of them already facing the vulnerabilities and prejudices inherent in being Alaska Native, should have felt safe within their own community, protected by those sworn to serve and defend. Instead, they were hunted by one of their own protectors, a man who had sworn an oath to uphold the very laws he so heinously violated. The uniform is meant to symbolize duty, honor, and selfless sacrifice. In Thomas Bunday's twisted hands, it became a cunning disguise for predation, a tool of deception that allowed him to move through the community undetected, his true nature hidden behind the perceived authority of his position. There is no true sense of closure in this case, only a bitter and enduring reminder that the badge itself does not inherently make the man – it is the heart and character of the individual beneath that uniform that truly defines them. Thomas Bunday may have worn the uniform with a chilling sense of pride, a symbol of the power it afforded him. But he killed with none – no honor, no remorse, only a cold and calculated disregard for the precious lives he extinguished and the profound trust he so callously betrayed.

-D. Boone Wilder

Chapter 8: The Isolation of Madness

The McCarthy Massacre

McCarthy. The very name evoked a sense of profound remoteness, a place where the tendrils of civilization seemed to fray and finally break. It wasn't simply a town tucked away in the vast Alaskan wilderness; it was, quite literally, the end of the line, the terminus of a rugged, unpaved road that dared to challenge the unforgiving terrain. Here, amidst towering peaks and sprawling forests, a hardy collection of souls lived by their own fiercely independent rules, their connections to the outside world tenuous at best, reliant on snow-covered trails carved through the wilderness and the fragile signals of crackling radios. In the spring of 1983, the town's meager population of just twenty-two residents was slowly stirring from the long, silent slumber of an Alaskan winter. The majestic Wrangell Mountains still loomed large on the horizon, their peaks capped with a stubborn crust of snow, and life in McCarthy had settled back into its familiar, quiet rhythm – a predictable cycle of survival and self-reliance.

That fragile peace, so hard-won in such an isolated and demanding environment, was shattered with brutal and terrifying finality when a stranger walked into their midst, not with a friendly greeting or a shared need, but with a rifle clutched in his hands and a chillingly singular plan etched in his deranged mind: to systematically kill everyone.

The Man with a Grudge

His name was Louis D. Hastings. A former newspaper editor who had migrated north from the perceived constraints of California, Hastings had come to the rugged expanse of Alaska in a desperate search for a freedom he felt had eluded him in the lower forty-eight. But instead of finding the solace and liberation he craved in the untamed wilderness, Hastings's heart had become a breeding ground for resentment – a bitter animosity directed towards the perceived ills of modern society, the relentless march of progress, and, most acutely, the very symbol of that progress in Alaska: the Trans-Alaska Pipeline.

AI Generated Image of Louis Hastings

In Hastings's increasingly fractured mind, the pipeline, an engineering marvel that brought vital resources south, had become the embodiment of everything he loathed, the entity he held responsible for the perceived ruination of Alaska's pristine wilderness. He became obsessed with the idea of stopping it. His mind twisted the problem into a horrifyingly simple and final solution: if everyone in the remote town of McCarthy died, there would be no one left to communicate with the outside world, no one to maintain the vital infrastructure, and therefore, the pipeline would inevitably shut down.

On the crisp morning of March 1, 1983, armed with a .223-caliber semi-automatic rifle, a weapon designed for rapid and efficient destruction, Louis D. Hastings embarked on his unthinkable and bloody mission.

The Massacre Begins

The first to fall victim to Hastings's deranged plan was Chris Richards, a resident of McCarthy who was shot without warning inside the presumed safety of his own cabin, his life extinguished in the sudden eruption of violence. Then Tim and Amy Nash, a young couple who had recently settled into their new home in McCarthy, their dreams of a life in the Alaskan wilderness cut short before they could truly take root, were gunned down in cold blood. Hastings moved quickly and methodically through the small, isolated community, targeting cabins one by one, his rifle spitting death into the quiet morning air.

He shot Les and Flo Clark next, an older couple who had spent decades carving out a life in the rugged isolation of McCarthy, tending their homestead with the quiet determination of those who understood the land. At some point during his deadly traverse of the small town, Hastings encountered James and Maxine Sherman. They too were met with the same brutal and senseless violence, their lives added to the rapidly growing tally of the dead.

In the span of mere minutes, six innocent lives had been brutally extinguished, the peaceful silence of McCarthy shattered by the unimaginable horror unfolding within its isolated borders.

But Hastings's rampage was not yet complete. He continued his deadly search through the small town, looking for more victims. He shot at Bob Maxwell, who, through sheer luck and quick thinking, managed to survive the attack by feigning death, lying still amidst the carnage as Hastings moved on. Another resident, Ronald Peterson, was also shot but, fueled by a desperate will to survive, managed to flee the scene on a snow machine.

A Race for Survival

Bleeding and terrified, the icy wind biting at his exposed skin, Ronald Peterson embarked on a desperate forty-mile journey through the unforgiving Alaskan wilderness on his snow machine, his only hope the distant promise of the town of Chitina. Bruised, frostbitten, and clinging to consciousness, he finally reached his destination, collapsing into the shocked and horrified arms of the locals who immediately raised the alarm, their urgent calls piercing the silence that had fallen over McCarthy.

Back in the isolated town, Louis Hastings found himself trapped, the possibility of further escape dwindling with each passing moment.

In a bizarre and unsettling turn of events, he encountered a young man named Jay Sidle and took him hostage. Yet, inexplicably, Hastings did not kill him. Instead, he rambled incoherently about his deluded mission to "save Alaska," attempting to justify his horrific actions with his warped ideology. Sidle, displaying remarkable courage and presence of mind in the face of mortal danger, played along with Hastings's delusional narrative, calmly keeping Hastings occupied until authorities arrived. When Alaska State Troopers, alerted by Ronald Peterson's desperate escape, finally descended upon the isolated cabin where Hastings held his captive, the scene was one of profound and unsettling stillness. Hastings, his rampage seemingly spent, offered no resistance. He was arrested without a fight.

Aftermath and Trial

The survivors and the bodies were transported through the frozen wilderness to hospitals and morgues. The tight-knit community of McCarthy, its population tragically reduced by nearly a quarter in the span of a single, horrific morning, was left stunned and broken. In the sterile environment of the courtroom, Louis Hastings displayed no flicker of remorse for the carnage he had unleashed. He continued to ramble about his twisted vision of "saving Alaska" and halting the progress of the pipeline.

The jury, however, remained unmoved by his bizarre pronouncements. They saw him not as a misguided savior but as a cold-blooded killer. He was convicted on six counts of murder and sentenced to a staggering 634 years in prison – a sentence that effectively guaranteed he would spend the remainder of his life behind bars. He remains incarcerated to this day.

Reflections from the Badge

You expect a certain level of danger in the bustling anonymity of cities, where violence can sadly become a grim part of the urban landscape. But McCarthy? A place where neighbors knew each other intimately, where they readily shared tools and resources, where they banded together to help each other navigate the long and unforgiving Alaskan winters? That's where the true horror of the McCarthy Massacre lies. The chilling realization that even in a place seemingly so pure, so removed from the perceived corruptions of the outside world, one man's twisted ideology could shatter the illusion of paradise and transform a peaceful sanctuary into a scene of unimaginable carnage.

Alaska is a land that draws dreamers, rugged individuals seeking to test their limits against the raw power of nature. But sometimes, tragically, the ones who come seeking solace are already deeply lost, dragging their inner demons along for the long and isolating ride. The McCarthy Massacre didn't just haunt the small community where it occurred. It left an indelible and unsettling scar on the collective psyche of every Alaskan who had once believed in the inherent safety and tranquility of their vast and seemingly untouched wilderness. A town of just twenty-two souls lost six precious lives in the span of a single, horrifying morning. And in the profound and unsettling stillness that followed, Alaska, as a whole, seemed to take a deep, mournful breath.

Reflections from Boone Wilder

The McCarthy Massacre serves as a stark and chilling reminder of the unpredictable and often incomprehensible nature of human darkness. In a place as geographically isolated and inherently peaceful as McCarthy, where the bonds of community were strong and life revolved around the fundamental principles of survival and mutual support, the very idea of such calculated and senseless violence seemed utterly impossible – until it tragically became a horrifying reality.

As an investigator who has witnessed the spectrum of human cruelty, it is often difficult to reconcile the sheer brutality of such crimes with the serene and often breathtaking beauty of the Alaskan landscape itself. Alaska is undeniably a place of vast and untamed beauty and remarkable resilience, but it is also a place where profound isolation can, in some individuals, tragically breed instability and distorted perceptions. Louis Hastings came to McCarthy ostensibly seeking peace and freedom, but he brought his own deeply troubled inner demons with him. Instead of finding the solace he craved in the quiet solitude, he found a twisted justification for his simmering rage, projecting his internal turmoil onto the innocent lives around him.

The McCarthy Massacre shattered more than just human lives; it irrevocably shattered the fragile illusion of inherent safety that many Alaskans, particularly those in remote communities, had long held. McCarthy's isolated and quiet existence had been its own form of sanctuary, a refuge from the perceived chaos of the outside world. But in that very solitude, Hastings, in his delusional state, saw not peace but an opportunity to manifest his warped and homicidal delusions. What remains most terrifying about this tragic case is not simply the brutal act itself but the sheer randomness of it, the horrifying way in which one man's deeply disturbed ideology led to such unimaginable and senseless carnage.

The aftermath of the massacre left the small community of McCarthy scarred, its innocence lost forever. Those who survived that horrific day were left with the immense and enduring burden of carrying on with their lives, of attempting to rebuild a sense of trust in their neighbors and their surroundings, and of forever honoring the memories of those who were so brutally and senselessly taken. In the end, Louis Hastings didn't just steal six precious lives; he stole the profound sense of peace and security that the community of McCarthy had painstakingly cultivated for generations in their remote Alaskan sanctuary.

Even now, decades later, when I think of McCarthy, I think not only of the horror that unfolded there but also of the quiet courage it took for those survivors to slowly reclaim their home, to find a way to move forward despite the immense weight of tragedy they carried. Alaska's spirit is undeniably strong, and its people possess a remarkable resilience in the face of adversity. But no one who knows the story of McCarthy can ever truly forget what happened on that cold March morning when one man's twisted vision turned a peaceful sanctuary into a scene of unimaginable horror.

-D. Boone Wilder

Chapter 9: The Cost of Courage

Remembering Troopers Scott Johnson and Gabe Rich

In the vast and often unforgiving wilderness of Alaska, a land where breathtaking, awe-inspiring beauty exists in stark contrast to a raw and ever-present isolation that can test the very limits of human endurance, the men and women of the Alaska State Troopers stand as far more than just law enforcement officers. They are the steadfast guardians of sprawling, often inaccessible territories, the unwavering protectors of remote and tightly knit communities, and enduring symbols of selfless dedication in a land that demands unparalleled resilience, unwavering courage, and a profound commitment to the well-being of others. Among their esteemed ranks were two brave souls, Troopers Scott Johnson and Gabe Rich, men who, in the selfless performance of their sworn duty, made the ultimate sacrifice. Their lives, though tragically cut short, embodied the very spirit of heroism that defines law enforcement in the Last Frontier, a spirit forged in the crucible of a demanding and often perilous environment.

The night of May 1, 2013, unfolded like so many others in the remote Alaskan interior – the air crisp and cold, the darkness a tangible presence pressing in around the small, isolated village of Tanana.

Nestled along the winding banks of the mighty Yukon River, Tanana is a community whose connection to the outside world hinges primarily on the unpredictable schedules of small aircraft and the seasonal passage of riverboats. The profound silence of the surrounding wilderness was typically broken only by the low hum of essential generators powering the small outpost of civilization and the occasional crackle of the police radio, a lifeline in the vast emptiness. It was on this seemingly ordinary night that Troopers Scott Johnson and Gabe Rich responded to a call, a report of a potential threat within the close-knit village. It was the kind of call that, in such a small and interconnected community, often involved familiar faces, misunderstandings, and situations that could be de-escalated with a calm demeanor, a listening ear, and a shared understanding. As they made their way towards the residence in the quiet darkness, neither man could have possibly foreseen the calculated malice, the simmering resentment, that lay silently in wait.

AI Generated Images of Troopers Johnson and Rich

The individual they were called to confront was Arvin Kangas, a man whose name was known within the small village, a name often associated with a troubled history and a volatile presence. As Troopers Johnson and Rich, partners united in their commitment to peace, approached his residence, they were met not with the possibility of dialogue, not with an opportunity to mediate or resolve a dispute, but with a sudden and brutal ambush, a senseless act of violence that shattered the tranquility of the night.

Kangas, armed and seemingly intent on violence, opened fire without any warning, the rapid succession of gunshots ripping through the stillness, instantly transforming a routine call into a scene of immediate and deadly peril. In that horrific and unforeseen moment, both Troopers were struck down, the violence swift, unforgiving, and utterly devastating. Their lives, lives dedicated to the noble cause of protecting others, were tragically extinguished in the very community they had sworn an oath to serve and safeguard.

The news of their untimely deaths ripped through the close-knit fabric of Alaska like a shockwave, leaving behind a profound and aching sense of loss that echoed across the immense distances separating its far-flung communities. Trooper Scott Johnson was more than just a law enforcement officer; he was a familiar and deeply respected figure within the Alaskan law enforcement community, a cornerstone of the principles he upheld. A veteran officer with years of dedicated service, Scott was known for his unwavering steady demeanor, his deep and abiding commitment to justice, and his genuine connection to the people he served. For Scott, it wasn't simply about enforcing the law; it was about being an integral part of the community, a reliable presence in a place where trust and dependability were not just valued but were essential for survival and harmony.

Scott was a devoted husband and a loving father, his roots running deep within the Alaskan soil, his life intertwined with the very landscape he served.

Trooper Gabe Rich was earlier in his career, his journey in law enforcement still unfolding with the bright promise of a dedicated future. Yet, in his relatively short time as an Alaska State Trooper, Gabe had already made an indelible mark on the hearts of those he encountered. His passion for helping others burned with an unwavering intensity, an inner fire that fueled his profound sense of duty and his unwavering commitment to making a difference. He possessed a genuine warmth, an infectious enthusiasm, and a ready smile that endeared him to the residents of Tanana and his fellow officers alike. To those who had the privilege of knowing him, Gabe was more than just a colleague; he was a friend, a young man full of boundless promise and unwavering idealism, a devoted husband and a loving father whose dedication shone through in every interaction, every call for service.

Together, Scott and Gabe were more than just partners on patrol, sharing the long hours and the inherent risks of their profession. They were a cohesive team, their individual strengths seamlessly complementing each other.

Scott's years of experience provided a steady and guiding hand, while Gabe's youthful energy and unwavering idealism brought a fresh and vital perspective to their shared mission. They were mentors to some of the newer officers, trusted friends to many, and for the people of Tanana, they were the very embodiment of safety, security, and the unwavering promise of protection.

In the agonizing aftermath of their deaths, communities across the vast expanse of Alaska came together in a collective outpouring of grief and unwavering support for the families of these fallen heroes. Candlelight vigils flickered against the somber backdrop of the long northern nights, their gentle glow a poignant testament to the light and hope that Scott and Gabe had brought to their communities. Makeshift memorials sprang up in Fairbanks, the hub of the interior, and in countless smaller towns and remote villages across Alaska, adorned with heartfelt flowers, solemn patches from fellow law enforcement agencies across the nation, and countless handwritten notes filled with sorrow, gratitude, and remembrance.

The subsequent arrest and legal proceedings against Arvin Kangas brought a measure of legal justice, holding him accountable for his reprehensible actions in the aftermath of the shootings, but no legal verdict could ever truly fill the profound void left by the tragic loss of Scott and Gabe.

Arvin Kangas was ultimately convicted of evidence tampering and sentenced to a significant term of ten years in prison for his actions following the shootings. However, the investigation revealed a heartbreaking and complex truth: Arvin Kangas's own son, Nathanial Kangas, was the individual who actually fired the shots that tragically took the lives of the two Troopers.

The subsequent legal proceedings against Nathanial Kangas culminated in his conviction in 2016 on two counts of first-degree murder and one count of evidence tampering. He was ultimately sentenced to a staggering 203 years in prison without the possibility of parole, a sentence reflecting the gravity of his violent actions and the profound loss he inflicted. During the emotionally charged trial, the devastating details of that fateful night were revealed: Nathanial Kangas shot Troopers Johnson and Rich as they were attempting to lawfully arrest his father on a misdemeanor charge, a seemingly routine encounter that spiraled into unimaginable tragedy. Arvin Kangas's conviction for tampering with evidence stemmed from his actions in the immediate aftermath of the shootings. In a desperate and misguided attempt to obstruct justice, he moved the Troopers' service weapons from the scene of the crime and wiped them down, actions that sought to conceal the truth and hinder the investigation. Although he did not directly pull the trigger, his deliberate actions to tamper with crucial evidence led to his conviction and imprisonment.

The killings of Troopers Scott Johnson and Gabe Rich sent shockwaves far beyond the immediate tragedy, deeply impacting the small and close-knit village of Tanana and resonating with profound sorrow throughout the entire state of Alaska.

The ensuing court proceedings were highly publicized, the details of the tragic events laid bare for a grieving public. The community of Tanana, bound by the unique ties of remote Alaskan life, grappled with a complex tapestry of emotions – profound grief for the fallen officers who had served them with such dedication, alongside complicated feelings towards the Kangas family, who were also members of their small and interconnected community.

As the seasons turned in the unforgiving Alaskan landscape, the heavy snows of that fateful night eventually yielded to the vibrant, albeit fleeting, blooms of summer. Yet, the enduring memory of Troopers Scott Johnson and Gabe Rich's selfless sacrifice remained, a solemn and poignant reminder of the inherent risks that accompany the profound honor of wearing the badge in the Last Frontier. Behind every star, behind every uniform, is a human being with hopes and dreams, with loving families who cherish them, and with a profound and unwavering calling to protect and serve their communities.

And so, as the midnight sun casts its ethereal glow over the rugged and majestic Alaskan mountains, we pause, we remember, and we honor their memory. We stand tall in the face of adversity, drawing strength from their courage and their unwavering dedication, just as Troopers Scott Johnson and Gabe Rich stood tall on that cold and fateful night in Tanana – the steadfast guardians of the Last Frontier, true heroes who served with honor and gave their all, right until their very last breath. Their sacrifice, etched into the very fabric of Alaska's history, will never, ever be forgotten.

-D. Boone Wilder

Chapter 10: The Girdwood Ghost

The Disappearance of Erin Marie Gilbert

The music was still playing when she vanished. A folksy band, maybe some bluegrass, the kind of tunes that weave through the trees at an Alaskan summer festival, lulling everyone into a sense of bucolic peace. The laughter was still ringing in the air, kids swinging hula hoops, the rich, earthy smell of kettle corn mingling with the sweet scent of blooming fireweed and the faint, unmistakable aroma of Alaskan summer rain. It was **July 1st, 1995**, and the Girdwood Forest Fair was in full swing—an annual kaleidoscope of quirky vendors, live music, and a general air of carefree revelry that epitomized the fleeting joy of a northern summer. It was the kind of festival where time melted, where inhibitions loosened, and where people let their guard down, perhaps a little too much.

Girdwood itself, nestled in the Chugach Mountains at the end of the Seward Highway, about 40 miles south of Anchorage, was a haven. A small, tight-knit mountain town known for its skiing in winter and its vibrant, artsy community in summer, it felt like a world away from the city, a place where people knew each other or at least assumed a shared sense of community. The fair amplified that feeling, drawing thousands into its leafy embrace, creating a temporary, joyous universe. No one expected a shadow to fall here, not in the bright glare of the midnight sun.

Erin Marie Gilbert: The New Alaskan Dreamer

AI Generated Image of Erin Marie Gilbert

Erin Marie Gilbert, 24 years old, had only been in Alaska a short while, but she was already carving out a place for herself. Originally from Martinez, California, she'd moved up to Anchorage to be with her older sister, Stephanie, and to start a new life, a fresh chapter in a place that promised adventure and independence. She was smart, with a quiet intensity, and possessed an artistic soul, often expressing herself through painting and writing. Friends and family described her as a gentle, trusting spirit, someone who genuinely believed in the good in people—even when, in hindsight, she perhaps shouldn't have. She sought connection, meaning, and the opportunity to build something new for herself in the Last Frontier.

She was beautiful, too. Thick, naturally wavy brown hair that framed a face with striking, intense eyes, and a quiet confidence that drew people in, making folks lean in when she spoke. She wasn't loud or flamboyant, but she had a presence, an inner light that was unmistakable. When she moved to Alaska, she embraced the spirit of the place, finding peace in its vastness, unaware of the lurking dangers that sometimes preyed on those who ventured into its shadows.

That day, she drove out to Girdwood with a man named **David Combs**, a guy she'd just started talking to. Not a longtime boyfriend, not even a casual dating partner. Just an acquaintance, someone she'd met at a bar in Anchorage a week or two before. He was a few years older than her, and while their connection was new, she seemed comfortable enough to accompany him to a festival in a town just outside the city. They were seen at the fair by various people throughout the afternoon and early evening—milling around the booths, watching a few bands on the stage, soaking in the quintessential Alaskan summer experience. And then… nothing.

The Unravelling: A Story That Doesn't Add Up

According to Combs's account, the car wouldn't start when they went to leave the fairgrounds sometime after midnight on **July 2nd**. It was dark now, though even in early July, Alaska's interior twilight lingered. He claimed he left Erin alone in her **1986 Dodge Spirit**— a relatively small sedan—to go get help at a friend's nearby house. He said he was gone about **two hours**.

Two hours.

Think about that for a moment. In a world before cell phones were ubiquitous, leaving a young woman alone in a disabled car, after midnight, at the edge of a bustling festival in a semi-rural area, is a decision that would raise eyebrows for anyone with a shred of common sense. Longer than most folks would ever leave someone stranded, especially a new acquaintance, in the woods, after dark. The Girdwood fairgrounds, while festive, could also be isolated in certain spots late at night. The parking areas were often dark, bordered by dense woods.

When he came back, David Combs said Erin was gone. Not just gone from the car. Gone. Period. No note. No indication of where she might have gone or why. Just an empty vehicle, an empty space where a vibrant young woman had been moments before.

That's when things started unravelling. Combs drove the disabled car back to Anchorage himself, after what he claimed was "getting help." He didn't immediately report her missing. It was Erin's sister, Stephanie, who became alarmed when Erin didn't return home and wasn't answering her calls. Stephanie, sensing something was deeply wrong, reported Erin missing to the **Alaska State Troopers** on **July 3rd**.

The Search: A Ghost in the Forest

The missing person report triggered an immediate and extensive search effort. Search and Rescue teams, helicopters, trained K-9 units, and dozens of dedicated volunteers—many locals from

Girdwood and Anchorage—converged on the fairgrounds and the surrounding wilderness. Girdwood isn't that big of a place, but the woods are deceptively dense, a mix of thick spruce and alder, riddled with creeks, bogs, and steep, brush-choked terrain. It's the kind of wilderness that can swallow a person whole, even in broad daylight.

They scoured the area for weeks, then months. They followed every possible lead, every faint hope. If Erin had simply wandered off, disoriented or injured, they would have found her. If she had decided to leave, someone would have seen her, or she would have made contact with her beloved sister. But the search yielded nothing. Not a shoe. Not a scrap of clothing. Not a fingerprint. Not a single, tangible piece of evidence that Erin Marie Gilbert had ever been there, let alone vanished from that spot. It was like she'd been erased, scrubbed from existence with chilling efficiency.

I visited that patch of forest once. Years after. Walked the same trails. Talked to vendors who still remembered the fair that year. You could feel it in the air—that wound that never quite healed, that unspoken question hanging heavy amidst the summer revelry. It was the kind of place where a ghost could truly feel at home, an absence more palpable than any presence.

The Cloud of Suspicion: A Shadowed Acquaintance

And when I asked about David Combs, the answers always came with a shrug or a raised eyebrow, a slight hesitation in the voice. The kind of hesitation that spoke volumes without uttering a single accusation.

"Never really knew the guy." "Strange he left her alone that long." "Wouldn't have been my first move."

Combs quickly became the primary focus of the Alaska State Troopers' investigation. He was the last person known to have seen Erin. His story, while consistent, simply didn't sit right with seasoned investigators or with common human behavior. Why would he leave her alone for two hours? Why didn't he report her missing immediately? Why did he drive the car himself, if it was disabled?

The Troopers interviewed him extensively. He cooperated, providing statements, and reportedly taking a polygraph test, the results of which were, as is often the case with such tests, inconclusive or not publicly detailed. He never wavered from his account. But without a body, without a crime scene, without any forensic evidence connecting him to foul play, the hands of justice were tied. The legal hurdles to prosecuting a murder without a body are immense. You need a compelling narrative of how and why the person died, and solid, independent evidence to corroborate it. The circumstantial evidence against Combs was strong enough for suspicion, but not for charges.

He was never charged. Never arrested. Never cleared either. Just that grey area where suspicion and silence shake hands, a haunting limbo where justice can't fully reach. The case remained open, but officially cold.

A Sister's Unwavering Fight: Keeping the Memory Alive

While the official investigation struggled against the cold silence of the wilderness, Erin's sister, Stephanie Gilbert, never gave up. Her fight to find answers for Erin has been a relentless, heartbreaking testament to sisterly love and unwavering determination. Stephanie became a fierce advocate, a tireless voice for her missing sister.

She posted flyers in every town, appealing to media outlets, launching a **Facebook page** that still runs today, nearly three decades later, continually updated with old photos, pleas for information, and messages of hope. She connected with other families of missing persons in Alaska, understanding their unique pain. She held vigils, organized search parties, and kept Erin's name in the public consciousness, refusing to let her fade into the snow, refusing to allow her to become just another statistic in Alaska's tragically long list of missing people.

Her efforts have been a constant, quiet battle against the erosion of time, against the fading of memories, and against the crushing weight of an unsolved mystery. She knows, as any family member of a missing person knows, that the case doesn't just go "cold" for the police; it remains a burning, agonizing inferno in their hearts.

But the trail grew colder with each passing year. And the years got quiet, the active search eventually tapering off, the public memory fading into the background.

Boone's Deeper Reflection: The Alaskan Ghost

There's something about vanishing in Alaska that hits different. It's not like disappearing in a sprawling metropolis, where you could simply lose yourself in the crowd. Here, the landscape itself is a character, an active participant in the story.

You expect danger here. Mountains that kill. Bears that maul. Blizzards that swallow you whole. There's a certain grim acceptance of nature's power. But what happened to Erin wasn't nature. It wasn't survival. It was something else human. Intentional. Calculated. It was a person, not a force of nature, who made her disappear. And that distinction is crucial and deeply disturbing. It speaks to a dark capacity for human cruelty that can manifest even in the most beautiful, seemingly serene places.

I've seen a lot of things in my time. The worst of humanity laid bare. But a woman like Erin, vibrant and full of life, doesn't just evaporate. She didn't walk away. She didn't get lost. Someone, or something, took her, and meticulously removed every trace.

The silence is the most insidious part of this case. It's a heavy, oppressive silence that blankets the Girdwood valley, a testament to a truth that refuses to be spoken. Somebody knows something. Somebody saw something. Somebody's stayed quiet too long, perhaps out of fear, perhaps out of complicity, perhaps out of a twisted sense of loyalty. And maybe they sleep well at night, convinced they've escaped justice.

But I hope one day, this state speaks back. Loud. Clear. With answers. I hope the relentless dedication of Stephanie Gilbert, and the memories of those who loved Erin, finally shake loose the truth from the silent earth. Because Erin Marie Gilbert didn't deserve to become a ghost, swallowed by the wilderness or by the darkness of another human heart. She deserved to go home. She deserved justice. And until that day, the ghost of Girdwood will continue to walk the silent trails, a chilling reminder that in Alaska, some mysteries are so profound, they become part of the very fabric of the land.

-D. Boone Wilder

Printed in Dunstable, United Kingdom